CAT'S GOT YOUR TONGUE?

A Story for Children Afraid to Speak

by Charles E. Schaefer, Ph.D.

illustrated by Judith Friedman

Gareth Stevens Publishing
MILWAUKEE

For a free catalog describing Gareth Stevens' list of high-quality books, call 1-800-341-3569 (USA) or 1-800-461-9120 (Canada).

ISBN 0-8368-0930-0

Published by

Gareth Stevens Publishing
1555 North RiverCenter Drive, Suite 201
Milwaukee, Wisconsin 53212, USA

Introduction for Parents, Teachers, and Librarians

At an early age, it is common for children to retreat to the safety of their parents when confronted by a stranger. Many parents and teachers have had to deal patiently with a young child who hangs onto them at family gatherings or who refuses to enter his or her preschool classroom. A number of kindergarteners and first graders are unusually quiet the first week of school while they become familiar with a new teacher, new children, and a new setting. However, some children, in spite of their physical ability to speak, continue their silence for months and even years.

This book was created as a learning tool for children who suffer from short-term or long-term stranger anxiety and for their families. Anna, who is diagnosed as an electively mute child, is the kindergartener in this story. She is treated sensitively and sympathetically; she is never punished or scolded because of her problem. Also, her behavior is never acceptingly referred to as "shy." Instead, the reader of and the listener to this story become happily aware of the positive aspects of speech, including self-expression and making new friends.

Not every child with stranger anxiety will refuse to speak outside the home and need the therapy that Anna did. But, hopefully, this book will make all these children feel that they are not alone.

Anna usually liked shopping with her mother, but not today. They found a pretty dress. Mama said it would be just right for the first day of school. The saleswoman put it in a bag and tried to hand it to Anna. But Anna just hurried from the store.

On the way home, they passed the school. Tomorrow Anna
started kindergarten. She didn't want to go.

When they turned the corner, Anna saw her little brother, Lou, playing ball with Grandma Garcia. "Come play, Anna," he called. Lou didn't have to go to school. He could stay home with Mama.

The next morning, Anna didn't want to get dressed. She *slowly* put on her new dress and her stiff black shoes. At the kitchen table, she stared at her bowl of cereal. "Anna, eat up," said Mama. "You don't want to be late your first day of school."

With Lou in a stroller, Anna and Mama walked the one block
to school. Anna dragged her heels all the way.

The school yard was filled with noisy children running, throwing balls, and playing hopscotch. Anna clung to her mother's hand. Then a loud bell rang. The children began lining up for class. Anna began to cry.

Her teacher, Ms. Spring, knelt down. "Say goodbye to your mother, Anna. Come on. I'll be your partner." Ms. Spring took Anna's hand and led the children into the classroom.

The children sat around long tables. They all gave their names, but Anna was too scared. She hid her face in her arms. Ms. Spring said, "OK, Anna, you can talk when you feel ready."

That evening, Anna's father asked her how she liked
kindergarten. "OK," she said. She didn't want to tell him
how scared she was. She hurried off to play with Lou.

A few days later, Mama said Anna would have to walk the one
block to school by herself. It was too cold for Lou to go outside.
That morning, Anna packed her stuffed kitten, Mittens, into
her school bag. After breakfast, they started to school together,
just as she had done with Mama.

Tucked into her coat, Mittens stayed with Anna at recess. Suddenly, Ronald ran over to get a runaway ball. "What do you have there?" he asked. Anna didn't answer.

"Cat's got your tongue! Cat's got your tongue!" he shouted as he grabbed Mittens and ran off. Anna ran after him. She grabbed him and hit him, trying to make him let go of Mittens.

17

When Ms. Spring separated the children, she asked what happened. Ronald blamed it all on Anna. "And what do you say, Anna?" asked Ms. Spring. But Anna just cried. Later that day, Ms. Spring gave Anna a note asking her parents to come to school.

The next day, when class let out, Anna's parents were waiting in the hall. Ms. Spring explained, "I am worried about Anna. She is not adjusting well to school. She has not spoken to me or to her classmates since school began." Ms. Spring said that the guidance counselor recommended they see a special doctor who could help Anna solve her problem.

The Garcia family visited the doctor's office that Friday. "Anna," said Dr. Linden, "I'd like to make it easier for you to talk to people when you want to." He smiled at her and her parents. "We can work together. Even Mittens can help." Anna didn't say a thing.

Anna visited Dr. Linden at his office every Friday after school. Dr. Linden read her stories. Then Anna drew pictures about the stories. Slowly, Anna began to talk about her pictures. Then about her family and herself.

Before long, Anna, Dr. Linden, and Mittens were putting on puppet shows. Their favorite was *Puss 'n' Boots.* "Anna, I bet your parents and teacher would love our puppet show. Would you like to show it to them?" Anna whispered, "Yes."

The next Friday after school, Dr. Linden, Anna, Mittens, and the rest of the puppet cast squeezed behind the classroom puppet theater. Anna peeked nervously through the curtain. Mama, Papa, and Ms. Spring looked funny sitting on the little chairs. Papa held his new video camera.

When the show was over, Mama, Papa, and Ms. Spring clapped loudly. They told Anna how proud they were of her. Dr. Linden said she was a star. He pinned a gold star on Anna's collar. "Thank you," she said.

25

The following week, Dr. Linden visited Anna and Ms. Spring
in their classroom after school. They talked about the puppet
show while they played checkers. Ms. Spring asked Anna if she
wanted to show the videotape to the class. Anna smiled and
said, "Yes."

On Monday, Ms. Spring played the tape for the class. Everyone clapped. Anna felt proud and happy.

Her classmate, Laurinda, rang her doorbell that afternoon. She was holding a box with holes in the side. "My cat had kittens," she said. "When I saw your puppet show today, I thought you might like to have a real puss 'n' boots. Your mom told mine it was OK." Anna and her new friend had fun playing with the little black and white kitten.

After that day, Anna began speaking more in class and making new friends. Now, when something new or strange scares her, she remembers her puppet show and how good she felt. Anna feels brave enough to speak even when she is afraid.

31

FOR MORE INFORMATION . . .

For Parents – Places to Write

Here are places to write for more information on how to talk with your child about dealing with fears and emotions.

The International Child Resource
   Information Clearinghouse
1810 Hopkins
Berkeley, California 94707
[This is a clearinghouse with over 10,000 pieces of available information, so if you write, specify the exact information you would like to receive.]

Children's News
Children's Hospital and Health Center
8001 Frost Street
San Diego, California 92123

For Children – Further Reading about Fears and Emotions

Every Kid's Guide to Handling Feelings.
   Berry (Childrens Press)
Feeling Afraid. Barsuhn (Childrens Press)
Getting to Know Your Feelings.
   Dombrower (Heartwise)

Sometimes I Worry. Gross
   (Childrens Press)
Stage Fright. Martin (Holiday House)
What are Feelings? Hazen (Forest House)

Glossary

anxiety: A feeling of being worried or nervous about something.

embarrassment: A feeling of being nervous or self-conscious.

emotions: Feelings all people have in reaction to certain situations. It is possible to experience more than one emotion at the same time.

guidance counselor: A person who is specially trained to talk to others about problems. Counselors try to offer sound advice to people in trouble.

imagination: The mind's special ability to think of situations and characters that don't exist in real life.

Index